Contents

Stealing the Hills

JOSEPHINE FEENEY

Level 2

Series Editors: Andy Hopkins and Jocelyn Potter

Pearson Education Limited
Edinburgh Gate, Harlow,
Essex CM20 2JE, England
and Associated Companies throughout the world.

ISBN 0 582 41797 X

First published by Penguin Books 1997
Published by Addison Wesley Longman Limited
and Penguin Books Ltd. 1998
New edition first published 1999

Set in 11/14pt Monotype Bembo by
Rowland Phototypesetting Ltd,
Bury St Edmunds, Suffolk
Printed in Spain by Mateu Cromo, S.A. Pinto (Madrid)

Published by Pearson Education Limited in association with
Penguin Books Ltd., both companies being subsidiaries of Pearson Plc

Introduction

We all looked at the picture of Mr Beech. 'The paper says that Mr Beech, a rich man from London, is going to buy the old mine,' my mum said. 'There'll be jobs for everybody.'

I wanted to know more about Mr Beech's plans for our village. What did he want to do here?

When they close the mine in Susan's village, everybody is sad. There are no more jobs. Then a rich man called Mr Beech arrives with a lot of money and a plan to open a new mine. He has other plans for the village, too. Most of the people in the village like Mr Beech. They are happy because now they have jobs again. But what is really happening? Susan and her friend Julie know.

Before long there is dirty black smoke over the village and the hills of their lovely Country Park. Mr Beech wants to ruin their village and steal their hills!

'We must stop Mr Beech!' Susan and Julie say . . . but can they?

Josephine Feeney was born in Leicester, England, but her mother and father are from Ireland. She worked as a teacher in mining towns for many years. This gave her the idea for the story of *Stealing the Hills*. In 1991 she stopped teaching and now she writes books for young people. Her first book, in 1994, was called *My Family and Other Natural Disasters*. In 1996 she wrote *Truth, Lies and Homework* and a year later she wrote *Stealing the Hills*.

Josephine Feeney lives in Leicester with her husband and their son and daughter.

Chapter 1 Getting Away From it All

When I was thirteen they closed the coal mine in our village.

A lot of people from the village worked there. My Dad and my two brothers were miners. Each day they walked up the hill to work. They worked far down, where they dug out the coal. 'It's hard work, Susan,' my Dad said to me.

When the mine closed everybody was sad. For years the miners worked hard to dig out more coal. Then, one Friday, my Dad and my brothers came home with a letter from the boss of the mine.

Dear Sir,
Thank you for working hard over the years.
I am sad to say that because we have no more money, the mine will close.
Good luck to you all,
Brian Overton

Eight hundred people worked at the mine. They all lost their jobs. Without jobs, they didn't have much money so some of the shops in the village closed down too.

With hundreds of others, my Dad went and looked for work. He was unlucky. 'I'm too old,' he said. 'I'll never find another job.'

My brothers went to Birmingham* and looked for work. My Mum and Dad were very unhappy about this.

All the young people started to leave the village. Mum and Dad were always sad. They never smiled. I felt unhappy so I liked to get away from it all.

My friend Julie and I went for walks in the Country Park. It is so beautiful there. It's a lovely place to go for a walk and get away from it all.

The Country Park is about a mile outside the village. If you walk

* Birmingham is a city in the centre of England.

When I was thirteen they closed the coal mine in our village.

up the hill in the park you can look down over the village. You can also see for miles and miles. It's a lovely place to sit and talk and forget about the world.

After the mine closed, Julie and I went to the Country Park every day. We walked slowly up the big hill and then sat up there. We looked down at the village.

'Everybody's very sad,' Julie said.

'I know. My Mum and Dad are unhappy because my brothers aren't here now.'

'My Dad has a lot of time at home now – he doesn't know what to do with it,' Julie said.

'We want more jobs in the village,' I said.

'Yes, jobs for everybody,' Julie said.

Then suddenly, there were lots of new jobs.

Chapter 2 Mr Beech Arrives

That was when Mr Beech arrived in the village.

Mr Beech drove into the centre of the village in his big car. He walked into the post office and spoke to everybody there.

Then he went next door to the bread shop where he spent a lot of money. Mrs Dale, the woman in the shop, put everything into a big box.

In the supermarket, Mr Beech spoke to all the workers and looked at the food. 'How's things?' he asked when he paid.

'Not very good,' one worker said. 'There's not much money round here. Not after . . .'

'The mine closed?' Mr Beech asked. 'Don't worry,' he said, and he put his things into another big box. 'Things will soon be different round here.'

I saw Mr Beech go into another shop. He bought a lot of meat and talked to people in there. Everybody smiled and laughed with Mr Beech.

Later that day, I was up at the Country Park with Julie. I told her all about Mr Beech. 'There was a rich man in town today and he bought a lot of things.'

'That's good,' Julie said. 'That will help some of the shops to stay open.'

'Yes,' I said. 'I love it up here in the summer. It's nice to look down over the village.'

'And the hills over there,' Julie said.

Then we forgot about Mr Beech, the man with lots of money. It was summer. Julie and I liked walking and walking. The sun was warm every day and we were very happy.

Then, one day, my mother opened the newspaper. She saw a picture of Mr Beech. 'Look,' she said. 'There's that nice man, Mr Beech – he was in the supermarket two or three weeks ago, remember?'

'Why is his picture in the newspaper?' my Dad asked.

We all looked at the picture of Mr Beech. 'The paper says that Mr Beech, a rich man from London, is going to buy the old mine,' my Mum said. 'There'll be jobs for everybody.'

'I don't know why he's buying the mine,' Dad said. 'There's no more coal under there. I don't understand.'

The next day everybody talked about Mr Beech. 'He's going to have a meeting,' Julie said. 'He wants to tell everybody about his plans for the village.'

'Do you want to go?' I asked.

'No. It won't be interesting!' Julie said.

But I wanted to go. I wanted to know about Mr Beech's plans for our village. What did he want to do here?

Chapter 3 New Plans for the Village

Mr Beech had the meeting in the big room next to the church. He stood at the door and smiled at everybody and said, 'Hello.' Inside, in one corner, there was a big table with lovely food on it.

When the meeting began, Mr Beech did not say anything. A

'There was a rich man in town today and he bought lots of things.'

young woman stood up at the front of the room. She was very pretty. As soon as she started to speak, everybody liked her.

She talked about Mr Beech's plans for the old mine buildings. Then she said, 'Mr Beech now owns the supermarket too. There'll be lots more jobs there.'

It was late now. People began to look at the lovely food. They were tired. Mr Beech's plans were not very interesting or exciting.

'One more thing,' the young woman said. 'Mr Beech is going to buy the hill next to the Country Park.' She began to put her things away. 'Thank you for listening,' she said.

'What for?' a man said from the back of the room. It was old Mr George. He was about ninety.

'I don't understand you,' the young woman said.

'Why is Mr Beech buying the hill next to the Country Park?' Mr George asked.

The young woman looked quite angry. She looked hard at Mr George. 'That's not your business,' she said.

'Oh yes it *is* my business,' Mr George said.

People wanted to leave. They were hungry. They wanted old Mr George to be quiet. They wanted to eat all the lovely food and go home.

The young woman looked at Mr Beech. He stood up and moved about. 'We're going to look for more coal there,' he said.

'There's no coal under there!' Mr George said angrily.

'There *is* coal,' Mr Beech said. 'And it isn't far down – we can dig for it easily.'

'What about our lovely Country Park?' Mr George asked. 'This will ruin our park and the hill!'

'No, it won't,' Mr Beech said. 'There'll be jobs for everybody too.'

'Somebody must stop you from buying that hill,' Mr George said.

'It's too late. I bought the hill yesterday!' Mr Beech said.

Mr George did not say any more. Everybody moved to the food

'Why is Mr Beech buying the hill next to the Country Park?'

table. Mr Beech and the young woman walked round the room. They smiled and talked to everybody.

'Are you hungry?' I asked Julie.

'No,' she said. 'Let's go and talk to Mr George. I'm sorry for him, he's over there.'

Mr George stayed in his place. He did not eat any of the food. 'He's trying to bribe everybody in the village,' he said. He was angry.

'What are you saying about the Country Park?' Julie asked.

'That man's going to take everything good away from this village. Then, when he has all his money, he'll leave,' Mr George said, sadly.

'I don't understand you,' Julie said.

'There will be big lorries all over the village. They'll ruin our Country Park,' Mr George said.

'We can't have that!' I said.

'Who can stop him?' Mr George said. 'He's buying everything and everybody and I'm much too old to do anything.'

'We can stop him,' Julie said. 'Mr Beech isn't going to ruin our Country Park.'

'Good for you,' Mr George said. 'I'm too old for him but perhaps you young people can do something.'

'We're going to stop Mr Beech,' I said. 'You watch us!'

Chapter 4 Lorries on the Hill

The next day everybody talked about Mr Beech.

'He's a good man,' my dad said. 'He's bringing money and jobs to the village.'

'Yes,' Mum said. 'It'll be nice when everybody's working again.'

'I don't like Mr Beech,' I said.

'Why?' Dad asked.

'Mr George says that he's going to ruin our village,' I said.

'He's a good man,' my dad said. 'He's bringing money and jobs to the village.'

Dad laughed, then he said, 'Old Mr George doesn't like things to be different, that's all.'

'No,' I said. I was angry with Dad. 'It's more than that. He'll ruin our lovely hill next to the Country Park.'

'Well, some people want a job more than a nice hill,' Mum said.

Most people said the same thing. In each of the village shops, Julie and I talked about the hills. Nobody wanted to listen to us. Mr Beech bribed everybody to be quiet. They all thought that Mr Beech was a good man.

Then Mr Beech started to look for workers.

WANTED
WORKERS FOR NEW MINE
GOOD MONEY, NICE WORK!
TELEPHONE MR BEECH ON – 0119 28756

Hundreds of people wanted the jobs. When Mr Beech drove round the village in his big car, people always smiled at him. They all wanted to work for him.

One day, in late August, Julie and I went for a walk in the Country Park. It was a lovely, summer evening.

'Look over there,' Julie said. She pointed to Mr Beech's hill.

We saw big lorries all over the hill. I was very sad.

'It's not too late to stop him,' Julie said. 'We'll make some posters. We must start tomorrow. There's no time to lose!'

Back at home my dad came in with his first money from Mr Beech. He gave it to my mum.

She looked at it and asked, 'Is that all?'

'Yes,' he said. 'That's all.' He was not happy with the money.

'But it's only half of what . . .'

'I know, but it's better than nothing.'

'But Mr Beech is very rich! He can pay you more than this,' Mum said.

'That's why he's rich, Mum,' I said. 'He doesn't pay his workers much money.'

The money was bad. The workers did not have any breaks for tea and only thirty minutes for lunch. It wasn't nice work. Before long the hills were black.

'I think you're right, Susan,' Mum said. 'Mr Beech is not a nice man! I can't buy all the food for the family with this money.'

'We must stop him, Mum, before he ruins our village,' I said.

Chapter 5 Save Our Hills!

Every day there was black smoke from the mine all over the village. The village was dark in the day and babies and children were ill because of the smoke.

Big lorries from the new mine drove quickly through the village. The hills were black but Mr Beech didn't look sad. He only wanted to steal our hills.

Julie and I met at her house. We made posters in all different colours. We wanted to stop the digging.

'MR BEECH IS STEALING OUR HILLS', said one and –

'STOP THE BIG LORRIES!' said another.

We asked the village shops to put up our poster. 'No!' they said. 'Mr Beech buys lots of things here.'

Nobody wanted our posters. We went home and put them in our front windows and in other places round the village.

The *Evening Post* took photographs of us. 'Things are going well,' Julie said.

People began to understand Mr Beech's plans. One man looked at one of our posters. 'You're right,' he said, 'Mr Beech is stealing our hills. Can I help you with your protest?'

A lot of people said the same as this man. People didn't like Mr Beech much now. 'I can't help you,' another man said. 'I don't like Mr Beech but I don't want to lose my job.'

In Mr Beech's supermarket, things were expensive. People didn't have the money to buy a lot of the things. Mr Beech tried to take

We asked the village shops to put up our poster.
'No!' they said.

everybody's money. He drove around the village and he smiled at everybody from his big car.

We had a protest meeting one Saturday morning. Julie and I made lots of posters for people to carry.

There was a lot of noise at the protest meeting. Eighty people walked through the village and past the Country Park to Mr Beech's hill. 'Save our hills!' we called.

At Mr Beech's hill there were a lot of men with big, angry dogs. 'Go away or the dogs will come after you!' Mr Beech cried.

'No!' I said. 'This is our Country Park! We're tired of you, you're the worst boss in this village! You're the worst boss in the world!'

'We want you to go away!' Julie cried.

'We want our hills back!' Mr George said.

'Go away, now!' Mr Beech said angrily. The dogs showed their teeth and made angry noises when he spoke.

'Let's go,' I said, quietly, to Julie. 'Those dogs are very angry.'

Julie turned to look at the people from the village. 'I think it's best to go home now. Mr Beech knows that we want him to leave the village.'

We walked back home and I was happy. After all this time, people in the village understood about Mr Beech.

A woman from the *Evening Post* newspaper was at the protest. She wrote down all about the angry dogs and the things Mr Beech said to the people when he was angry.

'You watch,' Julie said. 'Things will be different now. People now see what Mr Beech is doing.'

But Julie and I didn't know everything about Mr Beech. Before long I was very afraid. Mr Beech didn't like people to question his plans.

Chapter 6 Mr Beech Gets Angry

On Monday morning Mr Beech called at my house. His big car was in the street outside.

When I saw him at my door, I was very angry. 'What do you want?' I asked.

Mr Beech tried to push me into the house. 'Go inside!' he said. 'I don't want everybody to hear the things I've got to say to you.'

'No!' I said. 'Speak to me here, at my door.'

At first Mr Beech tried to be nice. 'Look, Susan,' he said. 'I'll try to be nice to you. I'll give you a job in my new shop. I'm being good to you,' he said.

'No,' I said. I left school five months before this and I didn't have a job, but I didn't want to work for Mr Beech. 'I don't want your job, Mr Beech!' I said.

'What about your friend, Julie? I'll give her a job, too. You'll work together,' Mr Beech said.

'No,' I said.

Then Mr Beech got angry. 'OK,' he said. 'How much do you want?'

'What?' I said. 'I don't understand you.'

'How much money do you want? Five hundred, a thousand pounds? You tell me how much you want,' he said.

'We want you to get out of our village,' I said. 'That's all. We don't want your money!'

'I'll pay you and your friend five thousand pounds to stop the posters and the protests,' Mr Beech said. He was angry.

'Mr Beech, you're trying to bribe me,' I said. 'We don't want your money. We want our hills. You're ruining our hills!'

'Don't you want the five thousand pounds?' Mr Beech said.

'No. It's a bribe!' I said.

'Fine,' he said. He walked to his car. 'You'll be sorry that you didn't take my money.'

Mr Beech tried to push me into the house.

Mr Beech pointed a fat finger at me. 'You wait and see what happens,' he said. 'You won't stop me, you know!'

Chapter 7 Things Get Worse

Mr Beech visited Julie, too. At half past ten the telephone rang. It was Julie. 'Mr Beech called at my house,' she said. 'He wants me to work for him.'

'Me too,' I said. 'I hope you told him to go away.'

'Yes, I did,' she said. 'What can we do now to make him leave our village?'

'Let's go to the Country Park this evening,' I said.

Julie said, 'Yes, that's a good plan. We'll talk about it then.'

Dad came home from work at one o'clock. 'What's wrong?' Mum asked. 'Why are you home early?'

'Mr Beech doesn't want me to work at the new mine now,' he said.

'Why?' she asked.

'Because Mr Beech doesn't want me working for him,' Dad said. He looked at me and his face was very cold.

'What?' I said. 'Why are you looking at me?'

'It's you, Susan! It's because of you! That's why Mr Beech doesn't want me to work for him now,' Dad said, angrily. 'Let Mr Beech get on with things, Susan. Don't question his plans!'

'He's ruining our village . . . and our Country Park,' I said.

'Susan, stop playing games!' Dad said. 'You can't give food to your family from a nice village or a Country Park!'

'I'm sorry about the job, Dad,' I said, 'but there's another thing you don't know about Mr Beech . . .'

A car stopped outside the front door.

'What about Mr Beech?' Dad asked.

'He's . . .' I began again. Then a brick flew through the closed window.

Mum cried, 'What's happening?'

'It's you, Susan! It's because of you! That's why Mr Beech doesn't want me to work for him now . . .'

I was afraid.

'What's . . .' Dad said.

'There's a paper round the brick. There's writing on it . . .' Mum said.

I read the paper. It said,

GET OUT OF THE VILLAGE NOW!
YOU ARE IN DANGER!

Chapter 8 Sudden Danger

Julie and I were afraid. That evening we walked to the Country Park but it wasn't the same as before.

'Somebody threw a brick through our front window today,' I told Julie.

'A brick? I'm sorry about that,' Julie said. 'Do you know who did it?'

'No, I don't,' I said. I didn't say anything to Julie but I thought Mr Beech had a hand in it.

'You must go to the police,' Julie said.

'The police know – Dad told them,' I said. 'That's another thing – Dad's job. Mr Beech told him to go.'

'What?' Julie asked. 'Why?'

'Mr Beech says he doesn't want Dad to work at the mine now,' I said.

'Because of what we're doing?' Julie asked.

'Yes,' I said.

'I'm sorry about your dad. Is he very angry?' Julie said.

'Yes,' I said, quietly.

We sat down at our usual place under a tree in the Country Park. It was quiet and lovely. For a minute or two we forgot all about Mr Beech.

Suddenly, a dog ran quickly up the hill. 'That's one of Mr Beech's dogs,' I said. I stood up. 'Get up, Julie! Get up, now!'

The dog ran at us. It showed its teeth – dangerous teeth – and made a loud noise.

We turned and ran down the hill. My legs were heavy and I was very afraid. The dog was after us. Then I fell.

'Get up!' Julie called. 'The dog will catch you!'

I stood up and looked at my leg – it was black and blue. I looked behind – the dog was only about ten metres away now.

'Run!' Julie said. She was in the street outside the park. Then, the dog got my leg with its teeth and I fell again.

'Get off!' I called.

Julie ran back to me. 'Don't move!' Julie said. 'The dog will soon go away. Don't move!'

I tried not to move but it was very hard. The dog did not want to take its teeth out of my leg. Then, suddenly, a man called the dog and it ran back up the hill.

'Help me, Julie,' I said. 'My leg . . . it's . . .'

Julie looked up at the man. 'I know him,' she said. 'He was one of the men with Mr Beech last Saturday.'

'How do you know?' I asked.

'I remember his thick glasses and . . . that blue jacket,' Julie said.

'Julie – my leg . . .' I said.

Julie looked at my leg. 'That's not very good. We must get you to the hospital, now!' she said.

'And then to the police,' I said. 'We must stop Mr Beech!'

Chapter 9 Two Different Stories

At the hospital, a doctor looked at my leg. 'This isn't very nice,' he said. 'What happened?'

'It was a dog,' I said.

'Your dog?' he asked.

'No,' Julie said.

'Whose dog was it?' he asked again.

The dog ran at us. It showed its teeth – dangerous teeth – and made a loud noise.

'We don't know,' I said. 'But I think it was one of Mr Beech's dogs – he owns the mine and the supermarket in the village.'

'That's interesting,' the doctor said. 'There are more accidents than usual at this time of year. Perhaps it's that new mine . . .'

I looked at Julie and she looked at me. So . . . Mr Beech was not a careful boss. That was interesting.

When the doctor finished, he said, 'You must remember to tell the police.'

'Yes, we will,' Julie said.

It was difficult walking to the police station. When we arrived at the door to the police station we met Mr Beech.

'Had an accident?' he asked, and he smiled.

'No,' I said. I was very angry. 'Your dog did this to my leg!'

'I haven't got a dog,' Mr Beech said. He turned and walked away quickly.

Inside the police station I spoke to a policeman. 'What happened to your leg?' he asked.

Julie and I told him the story about the dangerous dog in the Country Park and the man in the blue jacket.

'Wait a minute,' he said. 'Did you stay in the Country Park or did you try to get into the new mine?'

'We were in the Country Park,' Julie said. 'Why?'

'Because Mr Beech was in here five minutes ago,' the policeman said.

'We know,' Julie said. 'We met him in front of the police station.'

'And he says that you two tried to break into the new mine!'

'What?' Julie said.

'That man!' I said. 'That isn't what happened.'

We told the policeman our story a second time. He didn't listen to us. 'I think Mr Beech told the right story,' he said. 'You tried to climb into the new mine and a dog got you, so don't come crying to me!'

'Yes, but . . .' I said.

'There's the door. It's best for you to go,' the policeman said. Then he looked down at his book and began to write.

'Had an accident?' he asked, and he smiled.

We sat outside the police station, hungry, thirsty and very sad. 'That's it,' Julie said.

'That's what?' I asked, looking at my bad leg.

'That's it. We can't do any more,' Julie said.

'Who says?' I asked.

'If the police think Mr Beech is right, then . . .'

'No, Julie. Make no mistake – Mr Beech can't do this,' I said and showed her the bad cut on my leg. 'Before this I was quite angry – but now I'm very angry! We *can* stop Mr Beech stealing our hills.'

Chapter 10 A New Friend

Two days later, in the *Evening Post*, there was a photograph of the protest at the new mine.

'Look at this,' Mum said. 'Look, Susan, you're in the newspaper.' She smiled.

'That's good,' I said.

'It's not good. What will Mr Beech say when he sees this?' my Dad asked.

'You don't work for him now, remember?' Mum said. 'Susan is helping the village with her protests.'

Mum tried to talk to Dad, to tell him about Mr Beech. He was not ready to listen.

'Mr Beech's men threw a brick through your window, remember?' she said.

'And his dog got my leg,' I said.

'How do you know?' Dad said. 'How do you know that it was Mr Beech's dog? You tried to climb into the new mine. A policeman called at the door to tell me that.'

'But I didn't try to climb into the new mine,' I said. 'Julie and I went for a walk in the Country Park. Now, we can't go there. Our *best* place in the village and we can't go there.'

Julie and I were very sad. No jobs, no money and no Country Park in the evening.

I wanted the protests about Mr Beech to go on and Julie did too. But we didn't know what to do next.

Then, one morning, a letter arrived. It was from a man at the *Evening Post*. I took the letter to my bedroom to read, away from Dad.

Dear Susan,

I work on the Evening Post *newspaper. Somebody told me about your protests and about your accident in the Country Park. Can I talk to you about this?*

Please telephone me on 220695.

Thank you,
David North.

I telephoned David North in the afternoon. Mum and Dad were in the garden. The house was quiet.

'Susan? Thanks for telephoning me,' David North said.

'Who told you about my accident?' I asked.

'A friend,' he said. 'Dr Jackson – he works at the hospital, remember? How's your leg?'

'It's better, thanks for asking, Mr North,' I said.

'Call me David,' he said. 'Now I want to ask you some questions about your accident. Is that all OK?'

'Yes . . . David,' I said.

'Did you try to get into the new mine, Susan?' David North asked.

'No!'

'Did you play with the dog before it bit your leg?' he asked.

'No. We went for a walk in the Country Park. We like to sit in one place, the same place as usual, and look down over the village . . .' I said.

'Susan, listen carefully and don't tell anybody about this,' David North said.

'I won't,' I said.

'Ten children had accidents in the Country Park last week,' David said. 'Ten children! All because of that big dog.'

Then one morning a letter arrived. It was from a man at the Evening Post.

'Mr Beech's dog?' I asked.

'Yes – and about seven mothers with young babies think that their babies are ill because of the black smoke from the new mine,' David said.

'What can we do?' I said. 'Julie and I tried to stop Mr Beech, that's all.'

'I think I know how to get him,' David said. 'When can I meet you and Julie?'

Chapter 11 More Help

David North and his wife lived in a small flat near the hospital. Julie and I visited them at the weekend. David's wife, Mary, was a doctor at the hospital and – she told her husband about my accident.

'Come in,' David said. 'Find a place to sit down.' There were papers on every chair in the room.

'How can we help you?' Julie asked.

'We tried our best,' I said.

'What about the people in the village?' David asked. 'What do they think of Mr Beech?'

'Well,' I said. 'Some of them think he's a good man . . .'

'Other people think he's bad,' Julie said.

'My wife, Mary, knows Mr Beech,' David said.

'Yes. I met Mr Beech some years ago,' Mary said. 'I lived in a small village in the north. Mr Beech did the same things there as he's doing here . . .'

'Tell us more,' I said.

'The mine closed down. All the men and women lost their jobs and then Mr Beech drove into town,' Mary said.

'What happened then?' Julie asked.

'He asked everybody to meet and listen to his plans,' Mary said.

'Then?' I asked.

'He bribed everybody. Nobody tried to fight him . . .'

'Come in,' David said. 'Find a place to sit down.'

'Then?' Julie asked.

'The same as in this village – accidents happened, children were ill – very ill because of the black smoke.'

'Then what happened?' I asked. 'Were there any protests?'

'Yes . . . but the protests didn't work,' David said, sadly.

'Is that why you asked to meet us? You wanted to tell us to stop the protests?' Julie asked.

'No,' Mary and David said.

'Well, why are we here?' Julie asked again.

'One of my friends,' David said, 'works for a television station. He's a detective – a television detective. He goes round the country and listens to people, and the problems people have because of the things their bosses do to them.'

'Are you talking about Mr Beech?' Julie asked.

'Yes!' Mary said.

'Can you help my friend? He wants to talk to you, Julie and Susan, on television,' David said.

'I don't know,' I said.

'What's the problem?' David asked.

'It's Mr Beech,' I said. I looked at Julie.

'Mr Beech tried to bribe us,' Julie began. 'Then his men threw a brick through Susan's front window.'

'He's a dangerous man,' I said.

'We know,' Mary said. 'We know everything about Mr Beech, but when you tell the country . . .'

'Then people can see what Mr Beech is doing . . .' David said.

'And tell him to leave the village!' Julie said. 'Susan, we'll be all right.'

I thought about this for a minute. I wanted Mr Beech to leave but I didn't want my family to be in any danger. 'OK,' I said, 'when do we start?'

'This minute. I'm sending my friend your photograph from the newspaper. I'll tell him about the problem,' David said.

'Good,' Julie said.

'There's one thing,' David said, quietly. 'Mr Beech mustn't

know anything. It's better for us and for the village, so don't say a word!'

I was excited but afraid, too. Mr Beech was a dangerous man.

Chapter 12 Watching Mr Beech

The black smoke from the mine was very bad. People had their windows closed all the time because of it. Sometimes at one o'clock in the afternoon it was dark. People never laughed or smiled and big lorries from the new mine drove quickly through the village. It was dangerous to walk across the street in the centre of the village.

Julie and I never went to the Country Park because it was too dangerous so we sat and talked next to the river. Then the river turned black. The black smoke, the mine and Mr Beech ruined everything.

'Where can we walk now?' Julie asked.

'In our back gardens!' I said. I was angry. 'All the village is black and dirty because of that new mine!'

'Where's that television detective?' Julie said. 'We spoke to David North weeks ago about Mr Beech.'

Julie and I walked to the shops in the afternoon and watched Mr Beech. He stood outside his supermarket and smiled. Some people smiled back but others didn't look at him.

'Come along this street,' I said. 'I don't want to be near that man!'

We went across the road. Outside the bread shop a young man waited for the bus. 'What's the time?' he asked. He didn't look at us. He watched the supermarket and Mr Beech.

Julie looked at her watch. 'It's two o'clock,' she said.

'Who's that, outside the supermarket?' the man asked.

'Mr Beech,' I said. I looked closely at the man. 'Everybody knows Mr Beech.'

'So you're Susan,' he said to me.

'Yes.' How did you know?'

'Now tell me again – that man outside the supermarket is Mr Beech?'

'I saw your photograph,' he said. 'You were in the newspaper and my friend sent it to me.'

'Are you David North's friend?' Julie asked.

'Yes, that's right – and you're Julie?' he said.

'Yes,' Julie said. 'What's your name?'

'John Morton,' the man said. 'Now, tell me again – that man outside the supermarket *is* Mr Beech?'

'Yes,' Julie and I said together.

'Good – you see, Susan and Julie, I'm filming Mr Beech so I don't want you to say anything.'

We didn't speak for some time. Mr Beech walked up and down the street and smiled at people. John Morton filmed him.

'Does that black smoke come from the new mine?' John asked.

'Yes, it does,' Julie and I said together.

'Are people here getting ill because of the black smoke?' John asked. 'It's very thick and dirty.'

'Yes, children and babies are getting ill because of the smoke, John. Ask the doctor – he's always working now,' Julie said.

'And the old people,' I said. 'Mr George isn't very well and the village is very noisy now. It was a quiet, beautiful place before Mr Beech came.'

'Now, big lorries drive quickly through the village. They're very dangerous,' Julie said.

'I understand,' John said. 'Things are very different now. Let's go for a walk and you can tell me all about the new mine, the Country Park and Mr Beech.'

'It's a long story,' Julie said.

'Tell me everything,' John said. 'I want everybody to know all about Mr Beech!'

Chapter 13 Filming in the village

The next weekend John Morton arrived in the village with more people. 'Today,' John said, 'we're filming at the Country Park and

On the Saturday afternoon, Julie and I sat in the village square. It was winter now and a cold day.

the new mine. We'll find Mr Beech and ask him some questions.'

'Be careful,' Julie said.

'Mr Beech isn't a nice man,' I said. 'And his dogs . . .'

On the Saturday afternoon, Julie and I sat in the village square. It was winter now and a cold day. Most people were at home, away from the black, dirty smoke.

At three o'clock, John walked across the square. 'The dog got me,' he said, 'but I've got Mr Beech! We filmed him at the new mine with his big dogs.'

'Have you filmed the river and the black sky over the village?' Julie asked.

'Yes – and the children,' John said.

'Good,' I said.

'Now, tell me more about the day Mr Beech tried to bribe you,' John said.

John filmed Julie and me talking about the day Mr Beech tried to bribe us with money and a job.

'He wants Julie and me to be quiet so that he can ruin our village and the Country Park,' I said.

'He's taking everything out of our village,' Julie said. 'We want him to leave and take his dirty mine with him. We want all the children to be well again. We want them to be better!'

John looked at his watch and then at the man filming us. 'That's OK,' he said. 'Julie and Susan, thank you. We'll be back next week – can you help us again?' John asked.

'Yes!' we said.

Julie and I said goodbye to John and walked back home. We were excited. 'We'll be famous,' I said. I was laughing.

'Yes . . . and we'll tell the world all about Mr Beech. He *must* leave then!' Julie said.

'I can't wait to see this on television,' I said.

'I'm hungry,' Julie said.

'Me too. Let's go home for our tea,' I said. We were happy again.

Chapter 14 Dad Understands

Mum and Dad were unhappy when I arrived home. They didn't smile or look at me when I walked into the house.

'Where were *you* today?' Dad asked.

'Why?' I said.

'Answer me!' he said. 'Where were you today?'

'With John Morton, filming,' I said. 'Why are you asking?'

'Filming? Will it be on the television?' Mum asked. She smiled at me then. 'What's the film about?'

'It's about the new mine and Mr Beech,' I said. 'Is there any tea, please? I'm hungry.'

'No, Susan, there's no tea,' Dad said. 'Mr Beech closed the supermarket door to us today – we can't do our shopping there.'

'Why?' I asked.

'Because of you, Susan, again. Mr Beech says that we can't buy food from his supermarket because of the filming,' Dad said.

'And the car isn't working so we couldn't go to the supermarket in the next village . . .' Mum said.

'What about the bus?' I said. Dad didn't say anything, he was very angry.

'There's no tea tonight and no breakfast, dinner or tea tomorrow,' Mum said.

'I'm sorry,' I said.

'Please, Susan, *please, please, please* leave Mr Beech to his business.'

'No!' I said. 'Mr Beech is ruining our village – somebody must stop him. After the film, everybody will know about Mr Beech.'

'Did you think about this family, Susan? What about us? We'll be hungry because of you!' Dad said.

'We can catch the bus to the next village,' I said. 'Mr Beech can't ruin our village with the dirty black smoke from the mine, Dad,' I said.

'She's right,' Mum said. She put her hand on Dad's back. 'Susan's right. That man is ruining things for everybody in this village.' Dad didn't speak.

'Thanks, Mum,' I said. 'Tomorrow, I'll telephone John Morton and tell him about the supermarket.'

'Good,' Mum said. 'And tonight we'll buy dinner from the fish shop.'

'Lovely,' I said.

Dad sat quietly and looked into the fire. 'Susan – ask John Morton to visit my garden. The vegetables are all black – we can't eat them this year,' he said. 'I made a mistake about Mr Beech. I thought he was all right.'

'I'm sorry, Dad,' I said.

Now Dad knew that Mr Beech ruins everything. 'And it isn't only my vegetables – other people's vegetables are ruined, too. Our village *was* beautiful,' Dad said. He began to cry. 'Now, look at it! Why did he do it?'

'For money, Dad,' I said, quietly. 'All for money.'

'Yes,' Mum said, 'for money.' Dad was very sad and he cried quietly for some time. He loved his garden and his vegetables. Mum didn't go to the fish shop for our dinner so I was hungry when I went to bed. I was sad for my dad but inside I was happy – at last he understood about Mr Beech.

Chapter 15 Stealing the Hills

Two weeks later, on a Thursday evening, the hills near our village were quiet. There was nobody on the village square or in the village streets. The supermarket and cafe were shut. There was no black smoke from the new mine and it was hard to find Mr Beech. This was because there was an important film on television called, *Stealing the Hills*.

Julie and I sat in front of the television with our parents. On the film we told the story of our protests against the new mine, the black smoke and the big lorries driving through our village.

We watched Mr Beech running away with his angry dogs when John Morton asked him difficult questions. We saw the babies and children, ill because of the dirty, black smoke. Everybody heard about Mr Beech bribing the people of the village – our lovely village. On the television everybody said, 'This *was* a lovely village, a *beautiful* village.'

Before the film finished, it showed the hills next to the Country Park. Julie said (on film), 'Look, Mr Beech is stealing our hills and ruining our village. We must stop him!'

When the film finished Julie and I danced about. Now everybody – *everybody* in the country knew about Mr Beech.

Then I heard the telephone. 'It's for you, Susan,' Mum said.

It was Mr Beech on the telephone. 'Susan,' he said. He was very angry. 'You'll be sorry you made that film. You wait and see!'

Dad saw my unhappy face and so he took the telephone. 'No, Mr Beech, you'll be sorry. You'll leave this village tomorrow! No, tonight. Go now! We don't want you in our village!'

Chapter 16 Changes for the Better

On Friday morning there was a meeting in the big room next to the church. David North and his wife, Mary, were there. John Morton was there, too. Everybody said 'Thank you' to David North and John Morton for making the television film.

Mr George sat at the back of the room. 'Now, we saw the film – we all know about Mr Beech, but how can we throw him out of our village?' he asked.

'We can stop buying food at his supermarket,' Julie's Mum said.

'Yes, it's too expensive,' another woman said.

'We can sit in the road and stop the big lorries,' my Dad said.

'We can all stop working at the mine,' another man said.

'What? What about money for food?' somebody asked.

'We can all pull together – we can help our family and friends with money and food,' Mr George said.

Dad took the telephone. 'No, Mr Beech, you'll be sorry. You'll leave this village tomorrow!'

'Mr Beech tried to steal our hills but we stopped *him!'*

Everybody stopped shopping at the supermarket and all the men stopped working at the mine. Men, women and children sat in the road to the mine and stopped Mr Beech's new men.

Everybody wanted Mr Beech to close the mine and leave the village. The supermarket didn't sell any food because everybody went to the next village for their shopping. Mr Beech lost a lot of money – he left the village because he lost his money!

Now there is no black smoke over our village and the babies and children are well again. There are no big lorries so the village streets are quiet again.

A month after the mine closed, a new factory opened in the village. Julie and I work there, making dresses, jackets and coats for big shops in the city. Dad now works in a new shopping centre in the village.

The river is clean now and the Country Park is green and beautiful again. When we're not working, Julie and I often walk there and sit and look at our lovely hills. We talk about the protests against Mr Beech. 'We did it,' Julie says. 'Mr Beech tried to steal our hills but we *stopped* him!'

Yes, we stopped him. Now our village is happy and our hills are beautiful and green again.

ACTIVITIES

Chapters 1–8

Before you read

1 Look these words up in your dictionary. They are all in the story.
brick coal mine lorry meeting poster
Which word or words would you find:
a on a road
b under the ground
c on a wall
d in a big room (with a lot of people)
e in a wall

2 Now look up these words.
bribe business dig hill own protest ruin steal
a For which two words is money important?
Put the right words into these sentences.
b 'My sister ..... that CD now – she bought it from me yesterday.'
c 'I'm not happy about the new road, so I'm going to ......'
d 'Be careful with that red wine! You'll ..... your dress.'
e John went into the garden and ..... up some potatoes for lunch.
f Make sentences with the words *steal* and *hill*.

After you read

3 Write a sentence about each of these people:
a Mr Beech **b** Mr George **c** Julie

4 Who says this?
a 'Well, some people want a job more than a nice hill.'
b 'You're the worst boss in this village!'
c 'Don't you want the five thousand pounds?'

5 Where do these things happen?
a Mr Beech has a meeting with the people in the village.
b There is a protest meeting.

c A brick flies through the window.
d A dog runs quickly up the hill.

Chapters 9–16

Before you read

6 What do you think Mr Beech will do now?
7 Do you think Susan and Julie are in danger? What could happen to them?
8 Look at the picture on page 30. Read the words under the picture. What do you think is happening?

After you read

9 What does the doctor at the hospital tell Susan to do?
10 Why doesn't the policeman listen to Susan and Julie?
11 Why does Susan's dad think she tried to climb into the new mine?
12 How does David know about Susan's accident?
13 How does Mary North know Mr Beech?
14 How can David help Susan and Julie with their protest?
15 Where is John Morton standing when he films Mr Beech outside the supermarket?
16 Where does he film the next weekend?
17 What do Julie and Susan talk about on film?
18 Why can't Susan's mum and dad shop in the supermarket?
19 What does Susan's dad want John Morton to film?
20 Why does Mr Beech leave the village?

Writing

21 A year later television cameras return to the village. Write what John Morton says at the start of the film.
22 Mr Beech goes to a different village and does the same things. Somebody in that village starts a protest and telephones Susan for some help. Write their conversation.

Answers for the Activities in this book are published in our free resource packs for teachers, the Penguin Readers Factsheets, or available on a separate sheet. Please write to your local Pearson Education office or to: Marketing Department, Penguin Longman Publishing, 5 Bentinck Street, London W1M 5RN.